THIS BOOK BELONGS TO

This book has been specially written and published for **World Book Day 2016**. For further information, visit **www.worldbookday.com**.

World Book Day in the UK and Ireland is made possible by generous sponsorship from **National Book Tokens**, participating publishers, authors, illustrators and booksellers. Booksellers who accept the £1 World Book Day Book Token bear the full cost of redeeming it. (€1.50 in Ireland)

World Book Day, **World Book Night** and **Quick Reads** are annual initiatives designed to encourage everyone in the UK and Ireland — whatever your age — to read more and discover the joy of books and reading for pleasure.

World Book Night is a celebration of books and reading for adults and teens on 23 April, which sees book gifting and celebrations in thousands of communities around the country: **www.worldbooknight.org**

Quick Reads provides brilliant short new books by bestselling authors to engage adults in reading: **www.quickreads.org.uk**

EGMONT

We bring stories to life

First published in Great Britain 2016 by Egmont UK Limited The Yellow Building, 1 Nicholas Road, London W11 4AN

Illustrations by David M. Buisán

Designed by Richie Hull

Typesetting by Janene Spencer

© & ™ 2016 Lucasfilm Ltd.

ISBN 978 1 4052 8306 9

63701/2

Printed in UK

To find more great *Star Wars* books, visit **www.egmont.co.uk/starwars**

STAR WARS

ADVENTURES IN WILD SPACE

WILD SPACE

THE ESCAPE

CAVAN SCOTT

THE ESCAPE

It is a time of darkness. With the end of the Clone Wars, and the destruction of the Jedi Order, the evil Emperor Palpatine rules the galaxy unopposed.

Far away, in the unknown regions of Wild Space beyond Imperial borders, MILO and LINA GRAF accompany their explorer parents on their expeditions.

As the Grafs scout a remote and unmapped swamp-world, the shadow of the Empire draws ever nearer....

JF

CHAPTER 1

MARSHFIELDS

'Milo? Can you hear me? Come in, please?'

Lina Graf's landspeeder kicked up marsh-water as it sped across the swamp. Skim-snakes the colour of rainbows burst from the heavy canopy above, spooked by the engine. Through gaps in the branches, Lina could see that the sky was darkening, the stars obscured by thick clouds.

'Mistress Lina,' came a clipped voice behind her. 'Your parents won't be happy if you and your brother are still out after nightfall.'

'I know,' Lina snapped back, trying not to take her frustration out on CR-8R, the family's droid. She thumbed the comlink on the landspeeder's steering column. 'Milo, where are you?'

There was no response. Lina threw the landspeeder around a vine-covered tree, nearly sending CR-8R tumbling from the ramshackle craft.

'Careful, Mistress Lina!'

'I've told you a hundred times, Crater. Lose the "mistress". It's just Lina.'

'Yes, Mistress Lina.'

There was no point arguing with CR-8R, especially when she had a missing brother to find.

Beep-beep-beep.

A tiny red light blinked on the dashboard's locator screen. A smile spread over Lina's face. '*There* you are.'

It was a homing beacon, transmitting from Milo's speeder bike. He'd complained when their Mum fitted it, but she'd insisted for good reason. Nine-year old Milo was always running off. It wasn't

that he was particularly rebellious, but
he had definitely inherited their parents'
natural curiosity.

Auric and Rhyssa Graf were
interplanetary explorers, cartographers
who'd spent the last fifteen years
producing maps of Wild Space, an
unknown cluster of star systems on the
very edge of the Galactic Rim. It was
the only life Lina and Milo had ever
known. They had been born on the Graf's
starship, the *Whisper Bird*, and had grown

up exploring strange worlds ever since. Lina wouldn't have it any other way, but could do without having to repeatedly search for her younger brother every five minutes. It was always the same. They'd make planetfall and Milo would be off, hoping to discover a new species and become famous. His expeditions usually ended up with sprained limbs and a lecture from Dad – although they knew that he was secretly proud of his kids' misadventures.

But this trip was different. They'd brought the *Whisper Bird* down to this seemingly insignificant planetoid and set up camp in the middle of a vast rock-lined plain.

'You two, stay close to camp,' Auric Graf had said. 'There's a storm brewing and I don't want to have to chase around after you two when it hits.'

Milo had disappeared almost immediately, Lina receiving an urgent holo-message just a few hours later:

'Need your help. Come to the swamp, now!'

But where in the swamp? According to the *Bird*'s first sensor-sweep, the marshfields were huge, covering at least two-thirds of the planet's surface. This was typical of Milo – to get so excited that he forgot to give basic information, like where he was!

'Mistress Lina, the signal. . .'

'I see it, Crater,' Lina replied, watching the red dot trace across the screen. 'Almost there.'

Ahead, the landspeeder's floodlight glinted off metal. Lina slowed, bringing the craft to a halt.

Milo's speeder bike lay on its side in shallow water.

'Well, that's not going to help the paintwork,' CR-8R tutted as Lina leapt from her seat and splashed over to the abandoned speeder. She tried the bike's controls. They were dead, no power at all. What had happened here? Had Milo crashed?

'Master Milo,' CR-8R called out. 'Where are you?'

'Crater, shhh!' Lina hissed. 'This place could be crawling with razor-boars.'

'Well, excuse me for trying to locate your wayward brother,' CR-8R replied haughtily. 'I just assumed that's why you dragged me out into this abominable quagmire. For all we know, Master Milo is up to his neck in a sink-bog.'

'And if we're lucky we'll lose you in one too,' Lina muttered beneath her breath.

She didn't mean it, of course. CR-8R had been around Lina's entire life. He was one of her mum's pet projects, a mad mash-up of a droid constructed from a dozen different models. His base had been a probe droid, and it still had four manipulator arms that twitched as CR-8R hovered out of the landspeeder. His upper body was made up of a medical droid's waist welded to the torso of an astromech.

Not even his arms matched. The left was taken from an obsolete DUM-series, while the right was the shining silver limb of a protocol droid, but with interchangeable tool attachments instead of a hand.

Lina had no idea where Mum had found CR-8R's mournful chrome head, but knew that it was packed with information – most of it useless. For a brain, Rhyssa had used a protocol droid's processor unit, meaning that CR-8R had a tendency to be prim, proper and more than a little irritable at times. The patchwork droid had their best interests at heart. It didn't make him any less annoying though.

Lina righted the speeder bike. 'He can't have gone far.' She reached into the tool belt she kept slung around her waist and found a small cylindrical comlink.

'Milo,' she said into the device. 'We've found your speeder, but where are you?'

The only answer was a scream from beyond the trees.

'Milo!' Lina yelled, running through the dense foliage. Filthy water splashed up her legs, reeking like rotten rikknit eggs. She didn't care. Her brother was in trouble. Her brother was . . .

Laughing?

In the clearing in front of her, Milo was floundering around in a huge sludgy puddle, covered from head to toe in dark crimson mud.

'Milo?' she asked, feeling her temper flare. 'What do you think you're doing?'

Milo looked over at her, his muck-covered face splitting into a toothy grin.

'I almost had it, Sis!'

Lina's heart sank. 'Had what?'

Milo grabbed his long wooden staff and struggled to his feet. His face was the very picture of excitement. 'It was like a Sullustan ash-rabbit, but huge, with a ridge of spines–'

'Your message said you needed help,' Lina interrupted, icily.

'I do,' he replied, looking confused. 'To catch the ash-rabbit.'

'I thought you were in trouble!'

'Why would you think that?'

'Because, 99.998 percent of the time, you are!' CR-8R said, hovering into the clearing.

'Oh no,' moaned Milo, 'why did you have to bring Crater? He's sure to tell Mum and Dad.'

'Engaging lecture mode,' announced CR-8R, drawing another groan from Lina's brother. 'Master Milo, your parents specifically requested–'

Before CR-8R could finish, a small creature landed on top of his polished head. It had floppy ears and gangly arms that wrapped around the droid's face. CR-8R let out a cry of alarm, while both Lina and Milo snorted with laughter.

'I knew I would hate this place,' the droid complained, swatting at the creature with his manipulator arms. 'What is it? A sludge salamander? A horned billipede?'

'There's no need to get your processors in a twist,' Lina giggled, before trying to pull a serious face. 'Morq, leave Crater alone. You know he hates you jumping on him.'

The creature looked at the children with small orange eyes and cackled with glee. Morq was the family pet, a mischievous Kowakian monkey-lizard and the bane of CR-8R's existence.

'It's that no-good animal of yours?' CR-8R spluttered. 'I should have known from the stench!'

'You don't have any smell receptors,' Lina said, as Morq danced a jig on the droid's head.

'Which shows just how bad the thing reeks!' CR-8R insisted, firing a sudden spark from the electroshock prod attached to one of his many manipulator arms. The discharge hit Morq in the rear and, with a wail, the monkey-lizard bounded off CR-8R's head to scurry back up a tree.

Lina sighed. 'Good going, Crater. Now we'll never get him down again.'

'Serves the beast right,' CR-8R murmured.

Lina shook her head, trying not to grin. Someone had to behave like a responsible adult.

'OK, let's get Milo's bike onto the back of the landspeeder–'

'There it is!' shouted Milo, running from the clearing before Lina could stop him.

'Milo, come back!'

'It's the ash-rabbit, Lina,' he called over his shoulder. 'Come on!'

Rolling her eyes, Lina raced after her brother. 'Just once, he'll do what I say. Just once.'

But today was not going to be that day. She found Milo crouched behind a moss-covered rock. On the other side sat a small purple creature eating a marsh-fruit.

'That's the ash-rabbit?' Lina said, dropping down beside her brother. 'I thought you said it was huge?'

'Well, huge-ish,' admitted Milo, 'and you'll scare it away if you blunder about like a happabore.'

Milo raised his arm towards the

rabbit, and Lina saw that he was wearing their dad's wrist-mounted net launcher. Auric Graf sometimes used the conner net gun to snare alien creatures. Like most of dad's field equipment, Milo wasn't supposed to touch it, let alone take it from the camp.

'You're trying to *catch* it?' she asked.

"Course I am. How else are we going to study the thing?"

'Holographs? Bioscans? Like a normal person!'

'Nah,' said Milo, preparing to fire. 'Nothing like getting up close and personal to nature.'

Lina watched as her brother lined up the shot, but never saw him fire the net. Something snagged the back of her tunic and she was dragged up into the air.

CHAPTER 2

SNARED

Surprised by his sister's sudden cry, Milo's shot went wide, the net wrapping uselessly around a tree.

'Lina! It got away!' he moaned as the ash-rabbit leapt back into the undergrowth.

'Like I care!' came Lina's voice from above.

Milo looked up to see Lina hanging upside down, wrapped in barbed vines.

'What are you doing up there?'

'Getting up close and personal with nature!'

CR-8R crashed through the trees. 'Mistress Lina, you appear to have been

snared by creepervines!'

'I had noticed, thanks.'

'They're fascinating,' CR-8R added.
'Why, just three years ago, your father
recorded an incident where they
skeletonised a bantha in only . . .'

'Not helpful' snapped Lina, looking

up into the canopy. The creepers stretched down from a fleshy body with a wide, snarling mouth. She had to get free, but the vines were too strong.

'Where's my fusioncutter?' she said, feeling for her tool belt.

'You mean this?' Milo shouted up from the ground. He was holding a long tube-like device in his hand. It must have fallen out of her belt when the creepers had grabbed her.

'Throw it up to me.'

Her brother tried, but it dropped hopelessly back down. She was too high, and getting higher by the second.

'Crater, you try!'

'Gladly,' CR-8R said, snatching up the tool. 'Of course, the interesting thing about creepervines is that they largely hunt by sound. Remain quiet and they may lose interest.'

Lisa looked up at the open mouth that was getting closer with every passing moment.

'Not going to happen, Crater. Just throw it!'

Spinning a manipulator arm round like a propeller, CR-8R sent the fusioncutter soaring up to Lina. She stretched out, but the tool flew straight past her.

'Oops,' said CR-8R, 'I may have miscalculated the required distance.'

Lina watched as the cutter arced up into the canopy, only to be plucked from the air by a small bony hand.

'Morq!' Lina shouted in joy, as the rust-coloured monkey-lizard jumped down and landed on her legs. Nimbly avoiding a grabbing vine, Morq scampered down her body to press the fusioncutter into her hand.

Lina pulled herself up, fighting the pressure of her ever-tightening restraints, and fired the tool. She sliced through the creepers at her feet and felt the vines loosen, but there was no time to celebrate. With a cry, Lina and Morq crashed down, into a huge puddle.

'You OK?' Milo asked.

'No thanks to you,' Lina shot back, wincing as she tried to push herself up.

CR-8R whirred over to examine her throbbing shoulder. 'Mild bruising, that's all.'

'Doesn't feel mild,' Lina complained.

Pulling her tunic's collar aside, the droid gave the offending shoulder a quick blast with his bacta-spray. 'That should reduce the swelling until we get back to your parents.'

Lina looked down at herself. Her clothes were in tatters and she was drenched from head to foot. 'Mum's going to go crazy!'

'Not if she doesn't know,' Milo said. 'We can get changed before she even notices.'

Lina gave her brother a withering

look. 'And what about Crater? You gonna wipe his memory?'

The droid looked appalled. 'He most certainly is not!'

'Which is exactly why you should have left him behind!' Milo said, storming through the trees, Morq perched on his shoulder. 'No, in fact – you should have stayed there yourself.

At least then you wouldn't have made me lose the rabbit.'

Lina splashed after him. 'I made you miss it? Lo-Bro, you couldn't hit a sleeping rancor with a net gun!'

'Don't call me that!' Milo hated when she used the nickname she'd given him when he was little.

'Now, that's enough,' cut in CR-8R. 'Arguing isn't going to fix Master Milo's speeder bike or–'

The droid froze, both in mid-air and mid-sentence.

'Crater?' Lina said, concerned. 'You OK?'

'Receiving data,' the droid reported, his voice more stilted than usual. 'Processing.'

'Data? Where from?'

'Mistress Rhyssa.'

'From Mum?' Milo groaned. 'She's cross, isn't she?'

CR-8R didn't respond, but shook

his head as if trying to wake himself up.

'Crater, do you need to reboot?'

'No,' the droid replied. 'All my systems are working perfectly, thank you very much.'

'So, what's the data?' asked Lina.

'I'm not sure. It's heavily encrypted.'

'Decode it then!'

'What do you think I'm doing? The binary language your mother has used is positively archaic. No-one has spoken it in centuries.'

'Well, if you're not up to the job,' teased Milo.

'I am more than capable, thank you very much. It will just take time.'

'Time which we don't have,' said Lina, glancing up at the sky. 'We better take a look at your speeder.'

Milo's shoulders dropped when he saw his bike lying in the water. 'Oh yeah, I'd forgotten about that. I may have flooded the intake a bit.'

'And the rest,' said Lina, pushing past him to flip open the bike's access hatch. 'Look at it. There's marshweed all around the steering vanes, and as for the calibrators–'

'I get it, sis,' Milo said, his cheeks blazing red, 'I mucked up. Again. Let's just get it onto the back of the landspeeder. Mum will be able to fix it.'

'I'll fix it for you,' she said. 'That way Mum might not find out exactly how much trouble you got into. Dad's bound to have a spare repulsor array back at camp. Just help me get it onto the back of the landspeeder.'

Begrudgingly, Milo gave his sister a hand to lift the malfunctioning bike onto the landspeeder. It dipped worryingly and Lina hoped that its stabilisers would hold up to the extra weight. She had been on at her dad to replace the flying junk heap for months now, but, as always, he'd ruffled her hair and said that she could keep it in the air. '*My little chief engineer.*'

Of course she could – Lina had played in the *Whisper Bird*'s workshop ever since she could hold a hydrospanner – but that wasn't the point. Why did all of the Graf's stuff have to fall apart before they finally replaced it? It wasn't like they couldn't afford it, with all the credits they'd made over the last year or so. Since the end of the Clone Wars, people had started to travel further into Wild Space again, and travellers needed maps.

After making sure that the speeder bike was safely secured, Lina jumped behind the controls. Her brother was already hunkered down low in the passenger seat, still sulking that his expedition had gone so wrong. Morq was perched on Milo's shoulder, happily chewing a fleshy pink fruit, much to the disgust of CR-8R who was getting sprayed with pulp. Morq was a notoriously messy eater.

Just another day in the life of the Grafs, Lina thought to herself as she gunned the landspeeder's engine. *Wouldn't have it any other way. Most of the time.*

The landspeeder skimmed onto the plain where the Grafs had made camp. It was getting dark now, but Lina could make out the dome-like tents that CR-8R had constructed earlier. She peered over the speeder's windscreen.

'That's odd.'

'What is?'

'There's no lights.'

Morq immediately let out a concerned whine.

'Hey, don't worry about it,' Milo

said. 'The generator's probably packed up. I bet Mum's fixing it right now.'

The monkey-lizard nuzzled into him, not convinced.

'But I installed a back-up generator, myself,' CR-8R fussed in the back. 'Surely they couldn't both have blown?'

'We'll find out soon enough,' said Lina, as they made their final approach. 'After Dad tells us off, of course.'

'What do you think he'll make us do this time?' Milo asked. 'Clean out the *Whisper Bird*'s exhaust?'

'Worse than that,' Lina said, pulling a face. 'He'll probably make us listen to one of Crater's lectures!'

Milo let out a comic groan. "Please no, not the one about atmosphere-filtration turbines again. Anything but that!'

'Of all the cheek,' complained CR-8R. 'I'll have you know that A.F.T.

units are fascinating. Why, only the other day–'

'Crater, shut up!' Lina snapped.

'I beg your pardon!'

'I mean it. Listen.'

They fell silent, all straining to hear over the whine of the landspeeder.

'I can't hear anything,' said Milo.

'Exactly. Even if the generators are down, we should be able to hear Dad crashing about.'

She brought the landspeeder to a halt by the two domes and jumped out.

'Mum? Dad?'

There was no response.

'Where are they?' Milo asked, running up beside her.

Lina scooted around the main dome, but stopped short when she got to the main entrance, slipping slightly in the mud. 'I don't understand,' she said, her stomach clenching as panic started to set in.

'Where is everything?'

'What do you mean?'

'Look. All our stuff. It's gone.'

The domes were completely empty. No tools. No equipment. Not even their camp beds.

'Have Mum and Dad gone back to the *Bird*?' Milo asked.

'Without telling us?' Lina snapped, a little too forcefully. She saw Milo shrink back and forced her voice to be calm. 'It's not like them, that's all.'

Milo shrugged. 'Dad did say a storm was coming.'

Lina scanned the horizon, her fists clenched so hard that her nails were digging into her palms. She wasn't sure about any of this. The *Whisper Bird* was sheltering in a nearby cave system, but if their parents had headed back early, why hadn't they taken the domes with them? Nothing about this made sense.

Nearby, CR-8R swept his flashlight attachment over the muddy ground around the camp. 'Wherever they've gone, it looks like they had company.'

'What are you talking about?' Milo asked, running over to the droid. 'No one else is on this planet, are they?'

CR-8R shook his head. 'No. Dil Pexton said your parents have exclusive rights.'

Dil Pexton was the Graf's agent out here in the Rim Worlds, setting up deals for the maps and data the family made while exploring. He had been the one who'd put them onto this swampworld in the first place, a planetoid so remote that it didn't even have an official name. Dad joked that they could christen it 'Graf-World'.

'Could it be Dil?' Lina asked, desperately trying to keep positive.

'Not unless he's brought friends,'

replied Milo. 'Crater, shine your light over here.'

The droid pointed his light in the direction Milo was pointing. It revealed a host of large footprints in the mud.

'Loads of them,' said Milo, his voice wavering. 'And Dil's feet aren't that big!'

'What's that?' Lina asked, as something shone in the mud. She bent down and pulled out a long gold chain with an emerald star pendant.

'It's Mum's,' Milo said. 'Dad gave it to her on Morellia.'

'She wouldn't leave it behind,' Lina insisted. 'She loved it.'

'Unless she doesn't know she's dropped it,' CR-8R said.

'Wait, there's something else.' Milo dropped down on his knees, scrabbling around in the dirt. 'It's sunk right down.'

'Let me see.' Lina helped him pull the small device from the ground.

'It's the holo-recorder your parents use to create three-dimensional surveys of the landscape,' CR-8R said.

'Yes, I know what it is,' snapped Lina, 'but it's caked in mud.'

'There's a light flashing,' Milo said.

'It recorded something,' Lina said. 'If I can just clean the projector grooves.'

Using her sleeve, she rubbed mud

from the recorder. All of a sudden, it buzzed, light blazing from the indentations notched into its sides. Lina cried out in alarm, dropping the device, as ghostly glowing figures appeared around them.

'It's Mum and Dad,' Milo said as an image of Rhyssa and Auric Graf flickered into being in the mouth of the dome – but that wasn't all. Their parents were surrounded by a circle of armour-clad figures, each wearing a featureless helmet.

'Lina,' gasped Milo. 'They're stormtroopers! It's the Empire!'

CHAPTER 3

THE EMPIRE

N one of the holographic figures were moving, the life-size images frozen in a single point of time.

'Can you get it to play?' asked Milo.

'What do you think I'm doing?' Lina asked, cross-legged on the ground, a probe already jammed into the holo-projector.

It was eerie, being surrounded by the unmoving figures, like electronic statues, the plasto-canvas walls of the dome showing through their bodies. There was more to the scene as well. Just outside the camp hovered a hologram of some kind of Imperial transport, big and blocky, the image flickering as Lina worked on the projector.

Milo's heart hammered in his chest. This was *amazing*!

Even out in Wild Space, people sang the praises of the Empire. It was easy to see why. The Clone Wars had laid waste to the galaxy, with billions killed at the hands of the corrupt Republic. Now things were different. The Emperor had swept away the old order and was re-uniting the galaxy. With peace restored, the Galactic Empire was turning its attention to the furthest reaches of Wild Space, even out as far as the Unknown Territories.

'It'll make us rich, kid,' Dad had said. 'Just you wait and see.'

Milo wanted more than just riches. Mum, Dad and Lina could sell their maps and data-charts, but he had bigger plans. He wanted to join the Imperial Survey Corps, when he was old enough, and explore these mysterious new frontiers. Just the thought of all the species waiting to be discovered made his head spin.

Of course, he hadn't told Lina any of this. She would just laugh at him, but he was determined to make it happen.

Perhaps this was his chance. If the Imperials were on the planet, and already talking to Mum and Dad . . .

'I think I've got it,' Lina called over to him.

'Then what are you waiting for? Play the thing.'

She flicked a tiny control and the holo-recording started to move, the figures jerking into life.

'Now, Commander. You know, this isn't the way we usually do business.'

It was dad's voice, tinny, through the holo-projector's speakers.

'Crater, can you do anything about that?'

CR-8R swept up the projector with one of his manipulator arms and plugged it into his own system, amplifying the volume of the recording.

'*Times have changed since you left for Wild Space,*' said a stormtrooper with a tan-coloured pauldron strapped over his shoulder. Milo frowned. Even in a hologram, the stormtroopers looked impressive, standing there in their pristine white armour, but why were they clutching blaster rifles close to their chests? Surely there was no threat here.

'*Even so,*' said their mother, Rhyssa. She was looking as unsure as Milo felt about the situation, '*why we couldn't have met on a galactic waystation or–*'

A voice from behind Milo cut her off. Milo turned to see a figure silhouetted in the transport's open hatch. It was a huge man with broad shoulders, wearing a smart, functional uniform.

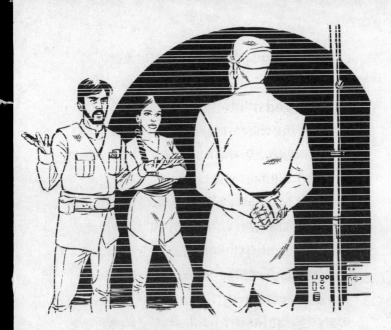

'*Cartographer Graf,*' the voice said, deep and commanding, '*where we have met is irrelevant. The only thing that matters is your data.*'

The spectre-like hologram of Auric Graf sidestepped the stormtrooper commander and moved toward the transport. '*Of course, Captain Korda. So, to business . . .*'

Milo felt a hand slip into his. Lina was standing beside him, looking nervous. 'Something isn't right here,' she said.

Milo pulled his hand free. He felt the same, but he wasn't going to pass up on the chance to bring his sister down a peg or seventeen.

'Don't be such a baby. Dad's laying on the Graf charm. This Captain Korda guy doesn't stand a chance.'

'Can I offer you gentlemen some refreshments?' Auric continued. *'Most of our supplies are back on the ship, but I'm sure we can rustle up a little Khormian brandy.'*

'That won't be necessary,' came the terse reply. *'You have the information I requested?'*

Rhyssa Graf joined her husband's side and indicated the datapad she held in her hands. *'All here, as agreed with our agent, Dil Pexton.'*

'And you won't regret it, Captain,' added Auric. *'New species of animals*

and plants, mineral deposits and natural resources for every planet in the sector, all with high-definition holo-graphics. The gold package.'

'I would expect nothing else.'

'Excellent,' Auric replied. 'Which brings us neatly to the next item on the agenda. Our fee.'

'Your what?' Korda asked, as if that was the most ridiculous thing he had ever heard.

Milo's dad laughed. 'Information is power, Captain, and power comes at price.'

At this, Korda stepped out of the shadows of the access hatch and, for the first time, the children could see his face. He had tightly-cropped light-coloured hair beneath a tight cap, his eyes small for such a large face, glaring at their parents from above a hawk-like nose. But what was wrong with his mouth? The Captain's chin was missing, the lower half of his face replaced by a robotic jaw lined with sharp metal teeth.

Milo grabbed his sister's hand and squeezed.

'*Cartographer Graf*,' Korda all-but snarled, stalking towards them, '*I am a Captain of the Imperial Navy. Trust me when I say that I understand power.*'

Milo wished that he could hide behind his parents, but that was impossible. They weren't really there, just tricks of the light.

'*I-I'm sure you also understand how this works*,' Auric was saying, his voice shaking slightly. '*We have something you want. You have credits.*'

'*No*,' Korda replied. '*You have something I want. I take it.*'

'*Not without a fair price*,' Rhyssa Graf cut in.

The Captain took a step towards Milo's mother. She stood her ground,

her chin held high.

'*You are loyal subjects of the Empire,*'
Korda said, his voice dangerously low.
'*You are obliged to hand over your data
immediately.*'

'*I don't think so,*' Auric said, giving
the stormtrooper's blasters a nervous
glance. '*Look, we're not Imperial citizens,
you can't order us around.*'

'*This planetoid is in Imperial space,*'

Korda pointed out.

'*Since when?*'

'*Since I made planetfall. Now, you can hand over your data willingly, or I can take it by force. It's your choice.*'

As one, the stormtroopers' rifles swung up.

CHAPTER 4

BETRAYED

The hologram cut off, plunging the children back into near darkness. 'What happened,' Milo cried out. 'Where did it go?'

CR-8R was already prising apart a corner of the projector. 'One of the memory crystals has come loose. I just need to slot it back in, and . . .' There was a click from the device. 'There.'

The holograms returned, but the action had moved on. Their dad was on his knees, his hands behind his head and a blaster levelled at him.

Milo ran over to his dad's image. Auric's face was swollen. 'They hit him.'

'*Now, shall we try again?*' said Korda.

Rhyssa's hologram sighed. '*You win, Captain. I just need to . . .*' Her voice trailed off as she worked the datapad, a tiny light flashing on its edge. There was a final beep and she held it out to Korda. '*Here. It's everything we have.*'

'*The right decision,*' said the officer, taking the pad and scrolling through its contents. '*The Empire thanks you.*'

'*You have what you came for,*' their mother said, trying to salvage a little dignity. '*I suggest you leave.*'

The Captain snorted. '*I don't think so. To become strong, the Empire needs to expand. Lord Vader himself has charged me with securing certain resources.*'

'*Like our maps.*'

'*Like* you. *For too long the talents of explorers such as yourself have been squandered on personal gain.*'

'*Now, wait a minute–*' said Auric

'*It's time for you to serve the Empire.*'

'*We'll do no such thing!*'

'*You have no choice. Take them.*'

The stormtrooper commander hooked a gauntleted hand under their dad's shoulder and pulled him up to his feet. '*You can't do this,*' Auric cried.

'*Is that so?*' sneered Korda, before turning his attention to the stormtrooper. '*Commander, I want no*

*evidence of what has happened here.
Strip this place clean and then take
care of the Graf's ship. Sensors indicate
that it's hidden in a cave system two
kilometres away. We can't blast it from
the air, so deal with it personally.'*

'*Yes sir,*' the commander
replied, throwing Auric to another
stormtrooper. More troopers had
grabbed Rhyssa and were dragging
her to the transport. She fought back,
her necklace falling from around her
neck to tumble to the mud. '*Korda,*' she
pleaded. '*You don't understand! Our
children are out there somewhere!*'

Korda's head snapped around.
'*Children? On this planet?*'

Milo felt his blood freeze in his
veins.

The Captain turned to the
commander. '*After you've dealt with
the ship, you'll find and deal with the
children. Understand?*'

'*No!*' Rhyssa wailed but was dragged in the transport by the stormtroopers. Their dad struggled but was soon overpowered. Forgetting that it was just a holo-recording, Milo raced forward to help – but when he reached out to try to pull the troopers away from his mum and dad, he found only empty air.

'*Get everything into the transport,*' the commander ordered, marching forward to stand on the exact point where they had found the projector. The image vanished in a burst of static.

Milo whirled around. 'No!' he shouted. 'Crater, do something.'

The droid shook his head. 'That's the end of the recording.'

The children stood in the empty dome, stunned.

'That was a joke, right?' said Milo. 'One of Dad's pranks?'

Lina looked at her mother's

necklace in her hand. 'Looked pretty real to me.'

'But how long ago did it all happen?'

CR-8R consulted the projector. 'There's no time stamp. It was damaged when the trooper trod on it.'

Lina looked up. 'No, wait. Remember when Mum was using the datapad, before she gave it to Korda?'

Milo realised what she was thinking. 'The light was blinking, like it does when it's sending data.'

'The information Crater received!'

'So it hasn't been long,' CR-8R said. 'We still have time to inform the authorities.'

'The Empire *is* the authorities,' Milo reminded him. 'We'll go to the ship.'

'To the *Whisper Bird*?' CR-8R asked. 'But the troopers are heading there!'

'We might get there first if we use the landspeeder. What do you say, Lina?'

Lina shrugged. 'I can't think of a better plan.'

'I can,' said CR-8R. 'Let's do something that doesn't get us blasted into a million pieces.'

'Just get into the speeder,' said Lina, running to the hovercraft followed by a still-complaining CR-8R.

Milo stood there for a moment, his head spinning. Everything he thought he'd known about the Empire was a lie, and now his parents were in their clutches. He had never felt so helpless.

There was a squeak from inside the dome. Morq was cringing in a corner, visibly shaking.

'Hey there,' Milo said, moving over to kneel with him. 'It's OK. It's OK.' The monkey-lizard let out an uncertain whimper and threw himself at Milo, wrapping his long arms around his neck.

'Yeah, I know. I'm scared too. But we can do this, if we stick together.

We need to get to the *Bird* before the stormtroopers. There's bound to be something in there that we can use. We've just got to be brave, OK?'

Morq hesitated, and then nodded, looking more apprehensive than ever.

The landspeeder slid in front of the dome, Lina at the controls.

'Are you coming, or what?'

'Yeah,' said Milo, carrying Morq to the speeder. 'Let's go.'

CHAPTER 5

THE *WHISPER BIRD*

'There's no sign of the stormtroopers,' said Milo, as Lina slowed the landspeeder to a crawl. In front of them a jagged mountain stretched up into the night clouds.

'It doesn't mean they're not lying in wait inside the cave,' CR-8R burbled from the back of the landspeeder. Morq let out a squeak and clutched Milo's neck tighter than ever.

'Keep quiet, Crater," Milo scolded. 'You're scaring Morq.'

'Forget that flea-bag,' the droid replied. 'I'm scaring myself!'

Lina killed the engine, the speeder

gliding to a halt. 'He's right though.
They could be in there, right now.'

'So, what are we going to do?'
Thunder rumbled overhead, the
first drops of the promised storm
finally falling. 'Stay out here and get
drenched? Come on, what have we got
to lose?'

'Our heads?" groaned CR-8R.

Clambering out of the landspeeder,
they crept along the bottom of the

mountain towards the yawning gap of the cave entrance. 'The *Bird*'s just in here. We're almost home.'

The sound of a voice in the cave stopped them in their tracks.

'Captain Korda, concussive mines primed and ready, sir. Detonation in T-minus 15.'

Lina pulled them back from the cave mouth, crouching behind large reeds.

'*Excellent work, Commander,*' Korda's distorted voice replied as four stormtroopers marched out of the darkness, led by the commander. '*And the children?*'

'Still missing, sir. But we'll find them.'

'*Make sure you do. Korda out.*'

The commander turned to his men. 'You heard the Captain. Scan for life-signs. They'll be the only humanoid life on the planet.'

'Sir, look!' said another of the stormtroopers, pointing at the landspeeder.

'That wasn't there before,' the commander said. 'They must be nearby. Fan out.'

Obeying his commands, the stormtroopers raised their blasters and started walking straight towards the children's hiding place.

'What are we going to do?' Milo whispered.

'Sneak past them into the cave?' Lina replied. 'Maybe we can deactivate the mines.'

'Or be blown sky-high,' added CR-8R, only to be whacked in the face by Morq's tail.

'We'll never get past them without being seen,' said Milo. 'Unless . . .'

Activating his net-launcher, he sent a net skimming low across the ground. It wrapped around a tree trunk,

disturbing a clump of tall reeds.

'Over there,' said the stormtrooper commander, changing direction to investigate. His men following, he approached the tree, brushing through vines that hung from the branches. Immediately, the vines sprung to life, wrapping around the commander. His blaster splashed into the marsh water as he was yanked up into the air.

'Creepervines,' Lina grinned. 'Good thinking, Lo-Bro.'

'Don't call me that,' Milo replied, although he was smiling too. 'Come on!'

At the foot of the tree, the other troopers took aim and fired into the branches. There was a horrible screech from above and the creepers went slack. The ensnared commander crashed down heavily into the marsh, but the children weren't watching. They were running for their lives, their heads down, towards the cave entrance.

Still on his back, the commander looked up and, seeing the fleeing children, swatted away his men's helping hands.

'There they are,' he yelled. 'Shoot them!'

The stormtroopers whirled around and fired, just as Milo and Lina leapt into the cave, CR-8R following close behind, his servo-arms flailing in panic. The shots hit the roof of the cave – and with a rumble, the entrance collapsed.

'Shall we scan for lifeforms, sir?' one of the stormtroopers asked the Commander.

The fallen trooper pulled himself awkwardly to his feet. 'No need,' he growled. 'If the rock fall didn't get them, the bombs will.' He glanced up at the dead creepervine creature in the tree. 'Come on, let's get off this mudball.'

On the other side of the collapsed entrance, Lina choked on the dust that had filled the pitch-dark cavern.

'Milo!' she croaked.

'I'm here,' he replied, from somewhere nearby. 'Are you OK?'

'I thought you would never ask,'

said CR-8R. The cave lit up as the droid activated his glowlamp. 'Get me out of here!'

'Are you stuck?' Milo asked, as Morq scampered over to examine the droid. CR-8R had been caught in a shower of falling rubble and lay partially covered by a pile of rocks.

'No,' said CR-8R. 'I've decided to have a little lie down. Of course I'm stuck!'

'We could just leave him,' Milo grumbled, beneath his breath.

'I heard that!' CR-8R yelled.

'I think you were supposed to,' said Lina. 'Alternate the current in your repulsor-circuit.'

'Why would I want to do that?'

'It'll create a vibration that might loosen the rocks.'

'Oh, yes, a brilliant idea,' the droid replied, 'if I want to get squashed flat.'

'It's either that or stay there until

your batteries go flat,' Lina said, reaching forward. 'Grab my hand and I'll pull you free. Milo, I'll need your help.'

Milo wrapped his arms around Lina's waist.

'Are you ready, Crater?' she asked.

'Not particularly.

'Tough. Do it!'

CR-8R's repulsors emitted a high-pitched hum, which was immediately followed by a worrying crunch from the rocks.

'Now, Milo. Pull!'

The children heaved, dust tumbling from the fallen rocks.

'He's not budging,' Milo grunted.

'He will. Keep. Going.'

All of a sudden, CR-8R shot out like a womp rat from its burrow, Lina and Milo falling back.

The droid hovered upright, brushing down his metal work. 'How

undignified, although I suppose I
should thank you.'

'I wouldn't yet,' said grimly, Milo,
pointing where rocks had fallen into
the gap. 'We're completely sealed in
now.'

'But at least we've got the *Bird*,'
Lina said, turning around. The ship
was exactly where their father had left
it, sheltering from the elements in the
large cavern. She looked more like her

namesake than ever, long bronze wings folded against the hull and landing gear extended, as if perched ready for flight.

As the children made for the ship, CR-8R hovered around the walls of the caves, checking the stormtroopers' explosive devices.

'Give us some good news, Crater,' Lina called, activating the *Bird*'s boarding ramp.

'I would if I could,' the droid replied, gravely. 'The mines are booby-trapped. One false move and they'll detonate.'

'So we either wait to get blown up, or do it ourselves?' Milo said.

'Or at least get buried alive. The devices are rigged to bring the roof down.'

'And with the entrance already blocked, we've no way of flying out before they explode,' Lina said. 'Today just gets better!'

'Who said we have to fly out?' said Milo, running up the ramp, Morq scampering at his heels.

Lina found her brother in the *Bird*'s cockpit working one of the rear consoles.

'What are you up to?' Lina asked.

In reply, a series of strident bleeps burst from the computer's speaker-grill.

'He's sending out a sensor pulse,' CR-8R said, peering over the boy's shoulder.

'Exactly,' Milo confirmed. 'Dad was planning to do exactly this before we left–'

'To create an echo-map of the entire cave system,' Lina realised as a three-dimensional holo-map appeared in the air between them.

'There,' Milo said, following the glowing tunnels with his finger. 'These stretch right below the swamp and out towards the mountains.'

Suddenly, his shoulders slumped.

'What's wrong?' Lina asked.

'I thought we could escape through the tunnels.'

'You mean, fly the *Bird* through them?'

Milo nodded. 'But this section here is far too narrow. We'd never make it through.'

'That's what Crater said earlier,' Lina reminded him, studying the holo-map.

'I'm afraid this time Master Milo is correct,' CR-8R said. 'The tunnel system is too narrow for the *Bird*'s wing span.'

'Then we'll just have to fly her out with the wings folded,' Lina insisted, swinging into the pilot's chair. 'Crater, plot the course into the navicomp.'

'You're joking,' Milo said. 'With the wings folded you'll only have the landing jets to keep us in the air. It's impossible.'

In response, Lina turned to CR-8R. 'How long before those bombs detonate, Crater?'

'Five minutes,' the droid replied, 'but—'

'So we have nothing to lose.' Lina grabbed the flight controls, and began flicking switches. 'Raising boarding ramp. Bringing engines online.'

Beneath their feet, the deck-plates rattled as the *Whisper Bird*'s sublight drive growled into life.

'Are you sure you can do this?' Milo asked. 'I mean, I know Mum lets you pilot this thing, but this isn't exactly open space.'

'In all honesty, I've no idea, but as the alternative is getting buried beneath a mountain, I'm willing to give it a go. What about you?'

CR-8R settled into position in

the co-pilot's chair, plugging his interface arm into the navicomputer. 'Personally, I think this is a dreadful idea, which probably means you'll do it anyway.'

'Something like that,' Lina said, trying to sound braver than she was feeling. Milo was right, this *was* impossible, but the alternative was unthinkable. She couldn't give in. Not now, not with Mum and Dad out there somewhere.

Swallowing hard, she pulled the control column towards herself. The deck lurched as the ship lifted itself from the floor of the cavern and began spinning towards the narrow entrance to the subterranean labyrinth beneath them. 'All set?'

'The course is plotted,' began CR-8R, 'although I must insist–'

'Crater,' Milo interrupted, strapping himself into the navigator's seat, 'we haven't time to argue. Do I think Lina is going to crash us into a cave wall? Yes. Am I hoping she'll prove me wrong? Definitely.

'Thanks for the vote of confidence,' Lina said, easing the *Bird* forward. With a blast from the landing jets, the spaceship disappeared into the tunnel.

There was no going back now.

CHAPTER 6

TUNNEL FLIGHT

'I have a really bad feeling about this,' CR-8R complained as the *Bird*'s hull grated against the edge of the tunnel.

'You're not the only one,' admitted Lina, trying to stop the ship from rolling. 'How long until the bombs go off'

Milo checked his chronometer. 'Two minutes. Maybe one.'

'Thanks for being so precise. It helps.'

'You just concentrate on getting us out of here in one piece.'

The cockpit shuddered as the *Bird*'s folded wings hit a crag.

'I'm trying my best.'

'Can you try it quicker?'

CR-8R cut in. 'Mistress Lina, the entrance to the next chamber is straight ahead.'

'I see it,' Lina replied, flying the *Bird* out into an enormous cavern.

Milo whistled, straining against his restraints to see. 'Look at this place. It must be miles across.'

'No time for sight-seeing,' snapped Lina, the *Bird*'s floodlights picking out two exits straight ahead. 'Crater, which do I take? The left or the right?

CR-8R consulted the map. 'The left leads to the surface, although it has to be said that the right-hand tunnel has a fascinating structure which suggests crystalline–'

A series of muffled explosions interrupted the rambling robot, followed by the sound of small rocks raining down on the *Bird*'s already battered hull.

'That'll be the mines,' Milo said.

'And *this* will be the entire system collapsing,' CR-8R added. 'We're going to be crushed.'

'The explosions have detonated, sir,' reported the stormtrooper commander as he joined Captain Korda on the Imperial shuttle.

'And the children?'

'They were in the cave.'

Korda's mouth pulled into a hideous grin that revealed more of his metal teeth. He turned in his command chair to regard Auric and Rhyssa Graf who were strapped to the cabin wall by arm and chest restraints.

Tears were pouring down Rhyssa's cheeks, Auric visibly shaking with rage. He looked like he would rip the Captain apart limb by limb if he could escape his bonds.

'There,' sneered Korda. 'No loose ends. Your old life is over. Now you serve the Empire. I suggest you get used to it.'

He pressed a toggle on the arm of his command chair, opening a com-channel to the shuttle's pilot.

'The children are dead. Take us up.'

'Hold on!' Lina shouted, banking to avoid a boulder half the size of the ship that had tumbled from the cavern roof. 'That was too close.'

Twisting the control column, she turned the *Bird* towards the exit on the right.

'What are you doing?' CR-8R wailed. 'I said go left.'

'I thought you said right.'

'I said the right was *fascinating*, not to fly into it for a look. Don't you children ever listen?'

'And don't you ever shut up?'

shouted Milo. 'Just do what he says, Lina!'

'I'm trying!'

Before she could correct their flight-path, a flock of large, purple-skinned creatures came swarming out of the crack in the cave's wall, screeching.

'Kinor bats!' yelled Milo. 'The explosions must have disturbed them!'

"Well, now they're disturbing me!' Lina cried as the *Whisper Bird* ploughed into the mob of thick, sinewy bodies. All they could hear was the beat of leathery wings, as the creatures thudded into the canopy, claws scraping against the transparisteel. 'I can't see a thing!'

'Left,' shrieked CR-8R. 'Take the left one!'

Lina grunted, her shoulder feeling like it was on fire as she swerved the ship to the left, flying out of the swarm. The *Bird* rolled into the clear exit, just as the colossal cavern's roof finally collapsed with the sound of a planet tearing itself apart.

'I hope you realise that we currently have a one thousand to one chance of survival,' CR-8R reported matter-of-factly. 'We'll never make it!'

'No, we will,' shouted Milo, following their progress on the holo-map. 'Lina, hard left. Now right.'

Lina followed Milo's orders, desperately trying to outrace the tunnel's collapse behind them. The ship bounced off walls, stripping heat plates and snapping antennae, but Lina didn't care. She just wanted to see the stars again.

'We're nearly there,' Milo cried, his voice all but drowned out by the roar of tumbling rocks.

'The gap's too narrow,' warned CR-8R, staring straight ahead.

'Then let's widen it,' Lina said. 'Milo?'

'Already on it,' her brother responded, undoing his restraints to switch seats behind her and pull down the targeting system. On the top of the *Bird*, the ship's mining laser whirled around, aiming straight ahead.

'Fire!' Milo shouted, and the rocks in front of them dissolved into dust just as the ceiling came crashing down.

'Chances of survival have just dropped dramatically!' CR-8R whimpered, shutting off his photoreceptors so he didn't have to witness his own destruction.

In a shower of rocks, the *Whisper Bird* burst from the side of a mountain. Rain hammered down on the canopy, but none of the crew complained. They were too busy cheering. Behind them, their hastily blasted exit caved in, closed forever.

With a flick of a switch, Lina unfolded the *Bird*'s wings and the ship soared high into the night sky. Milo flung his arms around his sister, who flinched in pain.

'Hey, watch the shoulder, Lo-Bro.'

'Sorry,' Milo said, untangling himself. 'But you did it, Sis. You really did it.'

'*We* did it,' she said, 'but we can celebrate later. Crater, where's that shuttle?'

The droid consulted the sensor array. 'It's already taken off,' he reported. 'Due to leave the planet's atmosphere in 30 seconds and counting.'

'We can't let them get away,' Milo said, sitting back in his seat. 'Mum and Dad are on that thing.'

'We won't,' Lina promised, pulling back on the column to bring up the *Bird*'s nose. The ship rocketed higher still, crossing the threshold into space in seconds flat.

'There it is,' Milo said, pointing out the lights of the shuttle.

'A Sentinel-class,' CR-8R reported. 'Capable of carrying up to 75 troops.'

'And prisoners,' Lina said, pointing the *Whisper Bird* after it.

'What are we going to do?' Milo said.

'I honestly don't know,' Lina replied. 'How's that mining laser?'

Milo checked his display. 'Barely functional. I think it took a knock blasting out of the tunnel.'

CR-8R's head swivelled towards the pilot's station. 'Mistress Lina, you can't be suggesting that we mount an attack? That class of shuttle is fitted with retractable laser cannons as standard, not to mention an ion turret, concussion missiles–'

'They've got Mum and Dad,' Lina bawled back, shaking with both frustration and fear. 'We can't just let them get away.'

Even as she spoke, the ship accelerated away at blistering speed. One moment it was there – the next it was simply gone.

'They've jumped to lightspeed,' CR-8R reported.

'That's it, then,' Lina said, slumping in the pilot's seat. 'We've lost them.'

Morq let out a sorrowful whimper, but Milo wasn't about to quit that easily.

'Don't say that, Sis. You didn't give up when Crater got stuck, or we were trapped in the caves. We can find them. I know we can.'

Lina turned in her chair and met her brother's gaze.

'You're right,' she said, a determined smile tugging at the corners of her mouth. 'Crater, how are you getting on decoding Mum's transmission?'

CR-8R cocked his head before replying. 'Package at 1.979 percent decryption.'

'Then keep working. In the meantime, set a course for Thune.'

'Thune?' Milo asked, leaning on the back of her chair. 'Shouldn't we head towards the Core Worlds? That's probably where Korda's taking Mum and Dad.'

'Yeah, but Mum and Dad have friends on Thune. If we're ever going to see them again, we'll need help and we'll need it fast.'

'The Graf kids against the Empire, eh?' Milo asked.

Lina watched as the co-ordinates scrolled across her monitor. 'Looks like it. And there I was thinking that the

Imperials were the good guys.'

'Didn't we all,' CR-8R mumbled from the nav-controls. 'And what do we do when we finally catch up with this Korda individual?'

'That's easy,' said Milo, ruffling Morq's hair. 'We improvise. Right, sis?'

'Right, Lo-Bro. Let's go.'

Lina punched the hyperdrive and the *Whisper Bird* leapt forward, into the stars.

READ ON

for an exclusive excerpt
from the next story

CHAPTER 1

POWER FAILURE

The *Whisper Bird* was in trouble and Lina Graf knew it. As soon as she'd brought the ship out of hyperspace, it had started thrashing around like a bucking bantha.

'Lina, what are you doing?' her brother Milo whined as he was almost thrown out of his seat at the rear of the cramped cockpit.

'Trying to fly straight,' she snapped back, flicking switches on the main console. Warning lights flashed on and off, and try as she might, the control stick wouldn't turn.

The ship shook, buffeting both children in their seats.

'You think that's straight?'

'Master Milo, please!' snapped the droid that was sitting to the right of Lina, linked directly into the navicomputer. 'Mistress Lina is doing her best.'

'And what if her best isn't good enough?' Milo grumbled.

'Then you being a back seat pilot isn't helping!' CR-8R insisted.

CR-8R, or Crater to his friends, was a patchwork droid cobbled together from a jumble of robot parts. Built by their mother, his body was an astromech's casing connected to a hovering probe droid base, complete with manipulator arms that whirled in the air as he spoke. He was fussy, argumentative and exceptionally annoying, but right now, he was also all they had.

Their parents were gone. Auric and Rhyssa Graf had been explorers, mapping the unknown reaches of Wild Space until they had been captured by an Imperial Navy captain by the name of Korda. Lina had always thought that the Empire was a force for good, that it spread peace and order across the galaxy.

How wrong could she have been? Korda had stolen their data, taken their parents and tried to blow up the *Whisper Bird* with Lina and Milo inside. They were alone now, with only cranky old CR-8R and Morq, Milo's pet Kowakian monkey-lizard, for company. Lina couldn't admit it to her younger brother, but she was terrified. No matter how much he blustered, she knew he felt the same way.

But for now, they had more immediate problems. The *Bird* had sustained considerable damage when they had escaped Korda's explosive charges and had only just held together in hyperspace.

'Coming up on Thune,' said CR-8R.

Lina glanced up through the cockpit's canopy, seeing a small brown and blue planet ahead of them.

'Are we going to make it?' asked Milo, hanging onto his seat as Morq hung on to him, wailing piteously.

'Of course we are,' said Lina. 'As long as the wings don't fall off first.'

'And how likely is that?'

There was a sharp crack from above, and sparks flew from the console's power indicators.

'Getting more likely by the second!' she admitted, wafting smoke away from her face. 'Crater, what's happening?'

The droid consulted the *Bird*'s fault locators. 'Where do you want me to start? Systems are shutting down all over the ship. The thrusters are overheating and life-support is critical!'

'What is working?' Milo asked.

'The food synthesiser is fully operational.'

'Brilliant. Anyone hungry?'

The sound of a small explosion echoed through the *Whisper Bird*.

'Actually, no,' CR-8R reported. 'It's just blown up!'

Lina felt like banging her head against the control console.

'We need to make planetfall for repairs,' she said, trying to hold herself together.

'Did you have to use the word fall?'

'Why not? If the repulsors give out that's exactly what we will be doing!'

'Life-support critical,' reported CR-8R.

'Will you just shut up!' shouted Lina.

'Don't blast the messenger,' CR-8R replied haughtily. 'I can't help it if the ship is falling apart around our audio sensors.'

Lina swivelled out of the pilot's chair and checked the readouts on the rear console.

'There's the problem,' she announced, bringing up a holographic display of the *Bird*'s engines. 'The main generator is failing, knocking out all the other systems.'

'Can you fix it?' Milo asked.

Lina had always been a natural with machines. When she was little she'd spent more time dismantling her toys than playing with them. The *Whisper Bird* was infinitely more complex, of course, but she could do it. She'd have to. With their parents gone, she was the eldest now. She was in charge.

She gave Milo's shoulder what she hoped was a comforting squeeze. 'If you help, I can.'

Milo broke into a smile and gave a mock-salute. 'Aye-aye, Captain.'

Lina grinned and turned to the

navigator. 'Crater, you steer the ship. Just keep us going forward, ok? Towards Thune.'

'Forward isn't a problem,' CR-8R replied. 'Any other direction and we may hit some snags.'

'You can do it,' Lina said, opening the cockpit doors and running towards the ship's engineering system.

'Oh, do you think so? How kind of you to say,' CR-8R replied sarcastically, as Milo followed his sister, Morq wrapped around his shoulders. 'I mean, I've only been flying starships since, let me see, BEFORE YOU WERE BORN!'

While CR-8R continued to grumble, Lina reached the main hold, Milo hot on her heels. She ran over to a ladder on the far wall and started climbing up to an access hatch set into the ceiling.

'I can get to the core through here,' she called down to her brother. 'Even if I can't get it working properly again, I can trip the back-up generators. They should supply enough power to get us down.'

'To get us down safely?' Milo shouted up. 'You forgot to say safely.'

'I can't promise that,' she said, reaching the hatch. 'But we'll be in one piece. Probably.'

'I hate probably,' muttered Milo, prompting a whimper of agreement from Morq. Above them, Lina pressed a control and waited for the hatch to open.

Nothing happened.

She pressed again, but still the small door didn't move. Trying not to panic, she flicked the manual override and tried to pull the hatch aside herself.

'What's wrong?' Milo called up.

'It won't budge,' she replied through gritted teeth. 'The mechanism must have jammed.'

'Is there another way in?'

Lina felt her heart sink. 'Yeah.' She clambered down the rungs.

'So, where is it?' Milo asked. 'How do we get in?'

'*We* don't get in,' Lina said. 'I do.'

'What do you mean?'

Lina moved over to a computer screen and activated a hologram. It showed a blueprint of the *Whisper Bird*.

'The generator is here,' she said, pointing at a flashing red light at the centre of the ship. 'And the jammed hatch is there.'

'OK, so how do you get past it?'

Lina swallowed. 'You use the external hatch, here.' She pointed toward a small doorway on top of the ship.

'External, as in outside?'

Lina tried to keep the fear from her voice. 'Yup.'

'We're in space, Sis. You can't go outside the ship while we're in space!'

'What do you think space suits are for? Besides, if I don't, we'll never land safely.'

Before Milo could respond, CR-8R's voice crackled over the comms-system. 'Mistress Lina, whatever you're going to do, may I suggest you do it quickly. The retro-thrusters have failed. We can't slow down.'

Lina slammed her hand against a nearby comms-unit in frustration. 'Change course then. Fly us away from Thune.'

'I can't. The controls aren't responding. If we can't change course very soon – I'm afraid the *Whisper Bird* is going to crash directly into the planet...'

Join Milo and Lina for more
ADVENTURES IN WILD SPACE – out now!

Book 1: THE SNARE
Book 2: THE NEST

WORLD BOOK DAY fest

Want to READ more?

SPONSORED BY
NATIONAL BOOK tokens

WORLD BOOK DAY
5 MARCH 2020

VISIT YOUR LOCAL BOOKSHOP

- Get some great recommendations for what to read next

- Meet your favourite authors & illustrators at brilliant events

- Discover books you never even knew existed!

FIND YOUR LOCAL BOOKSHOP
www.booksellers.org.uk/bookshopsearch

JOIN YOUR LOCAL LIBRARY

You can browse and borrow from a HUGE selection of books and get recommendations of what to read next from expert librarians—all for **FREE**! You can also discover libraries' wonderful children's and family reading activities.

FIND YOUR LOCAL LIBRARY
www.findalibrary.co.uk

GET ONLINE

VISIT **WORLDBOOKDAY.COM** TO DISCOVER A WHOLE NEW WORLD OF BOOKS!

- Downloads and activities for top books and authors
- Cool games, trailers and videos
- Author events in your area
- News, competitions and new books—all in a FREE monthly email

AND MORE!